Our Idiosyncrasies

FLASH FICTION & ESSAYS

Our Idiosyncrasies

Published by Chameleon Publishing

www.sanoberirshad.com

Illustrations by Shazia Alam

Our Idiosyncrasies

FLASH FICTION & ESSAYS

Sanober H. Irshad

"These were fun, engaging, interesting, and wonderfully written. The stories come off the pages with visuals in the scenes and a tone to help readers to immerse as they unfold."

- Marni MacRae,
International Award winning author

Table of Contents

Acknowledgements

Even though writing has always been my passion, besides board games, of course. I had never thought that I would end up compiling my writings into a book.

First of all, I would like to thank my husband, parents, family, and friends for their endless support. Especially my sister, Sadaf, for being my critic, reading through every word I wrote and giving her constructive advice, which I sometimes ignored.

For my son Aryan. I am sure he will fish for his name in the stories too.

Lastly, I would like to thank you for picking up this book and deciding to give my stories a read. I hope you enjoy my writing and take it with a pinch of salt.

The Perfect Match

Let me introduce you to a significant person in our society.

She comes in all shapes and sizes and carries along with her a big black book with the names of those who have either been unfortunate in love or claim to have never found it. You probably know her already; the rishtay wali aunty[1] — roughly translated as the matchmaker aunty.

Matchmaking, for us, is a complex issue. It usually involves the entire family. By entire I mean uncles, aunts, their kids, their neighbours, great grandparents, distant acquaintances, plus anyone who in one way or other shares our genetics or merely crosses our path.

[1] *Rishtay wali aunty* - A woman matchmaker.

The trend of finding one's soulmate solely through one's efforts, through the Internet, in the classroom, or at parties, has already caught on. However, there are still a few in denial that the institution of marriage exists. Usually, it's those who end up in that big black book of fate.

Still, it was different for my dear friend, Mia Shayan, an up-to-the-minute, well-dressed finance executive in Dubai. Her aim in life was to live it to the fullest. She was brought up to be independent and excel at everything, encouraged to be different and to fight for what she believed in. But all the values instilled in her by her parents backfired when they realised how emotionally and financially independent she had become; now unable to be forced into a co-dependent relationship.

Mia was a girl who hated clichés, but, somehow, she had become a perfect one.

It all started with her turning twenty-eight. Not married yet and twenty-eight! It is like a curse in our culture. Mothers start getting worried as soon as their daughters turn twenty-three. They frantically begin to socialise, talk to people, and fake smile even at those they secretly wish dead. After all, they have an eligible daughter who they need to fix up fast.

On the other hand, boys have a grace period of around five years to tie the knot after turning thirty. They can quickly get out of the pressure by saying, “I can’t handle responsibilities right now.” However, this statement also has an expiration date, after which; their marital status becomes a matter of concern within the social circle.

Getting back to Mia, being the only child, she had a lot more to prove. She wasn’t interested in falling in love, despite quite a few opportunities.

Her parents had already started looking for that perfect man who would gladly accept their 'over the hill' daughter and live happily ever after with her. Many months passed by, and their desperation increased. They had registered her with all the matrimonial websites and rishtay wali aunties they could find.

One day, my phone rang. To my surprise, it was Mia's mum. My intuition had already warned me about the caller's motive. "Dear, you know we have been looking high and low for a son-in-law," she said, "Mia doesn't seem to like anyone we bring. Do you think there is someone she is in love with?"

The question was a bit sudden. I didn't know what to say. I knew my friend was definitely interested in men, but not to the extent of falling in love. For a moment, I went back in time. I tried to remember if Mia had ever mentioned anyone in particular she had ever liked.

"No, Aunty. I don't think she is seeing anyone," I promptly replied before her mum, being an old-fashioned lady who only believed in arranged marriages, fainted.

The conversation with her mother on what Mia wanted out of life and how she had avoided settling down lasted for almost an hour, till I finally found a reason to hang up the phone.

For our society, thriving in life is not earning well, living in a beautiful apartment, or spending lavishly even during this period of recession. It's all about getting married and reproducing.

To make Mia understand her parents' point of view, I rang up my poor friend, who had been avoiding her mum's calls at work. I was stunned to find out the number of matrimonial websites she was registered on. According to her, there were so many prospective husbands to shortlist, and, amusingly, no one was up to the standard.

It was a little hard to believe until I saw the photographs myself. Mia was right. They were the funniest pictures I had seen that day. One stood like a Bollywood star, with arms crossed and right foot on a chair, looking into the camera, smiling like a criminal. Then, one posed with a strict face wearing specs as if his PHD course books were stolen.

Days turned into months, but no one seemed even close to being suitable for her. Her parents' anxiety for a groom spread like a virus, which eventually infected Mia.

Once, in a desperate attempt to alter something about her life, she stopped by the salon on her way back from work to change her hair colour.

Sitting there, she got so paranoid that she ran out of the salon with unwashed hair and still wearing the shower cap just so that she could get home in time to go through some profiles a matchmaker aunty had sent earlier.

There were many incidents like this, including an unfruitful visit to a shrink.

So, before Mia goes completely insane, if you know of anyone who is equally eccentric, settled, cute, and of course; desperate, then please drop in a line. It's not me, it's the society speaking, for they won't let her live in peace.

The Totka Factory

Desi[2] Totkas are like bittersweet dark chocolate; it just appears in your fridge in some form or another, and all you have to do is learn to enjoy or ignore it.

In ancient times, totka was actually a word used for witchcraft. Now, this sorcery has evolved into a much more simplistic form.

Every household comes equipped with a totka giving aunty—one who carries a plethora of knowledge, the art of intruding into everyone's life, and a magic potion for every problem in the world. Got sunburnt? Can't reproduce? Hair falling out? All you need is a totka aunty's attention and a few herbs and spices from the kitchen to do the trick.

---

2 Local or anything belonging to the Subcontinent.

So, let's get to our little story. It was a hot summer afternoon in Multan. Lamis was sitting in some upscale salon waiting for her over-the-hill bride friend to get all glammed up for the engagement ceremony.

The salon was rather empty and well lit up. Lamis sat in the airconditioned, glass doored waiting room, right next to the makeup studio, overlooking a beautiful, lush, green garden, oblivious to the hot and humid temperature outside.

The relaxing atmosphere had just started to sink in when, suddenly, a toddler barged into the room, screaming at the top of his lungs, almost breaking the ornate vase kept on the coffee table.

"Taha, stop it!" Screaming louder than the child, a lady dressed up like a runaway bride entered the room. "Sorry, he's just a bit hyper today. I think he has a sugar rush," she sheepishly explained, trying to get a hold of her toddler.

"So many remedies I gave you to calm him down, but you don't listen to me," grumbled an old lady entering the room.

The ladies exchanged a few greetings, and Lamis got an introduction. Umaiza, the woman dressed as a runaway bride, was waiting for her sister, the actual bride, to get ready for her wedding. She was accompanied by her aunt and two-year-old son.

After ten minutes of complete silence and uncomfortable stares, Aunty finally questioned, "So, Lamis beta[3], are you married?"

"Jee[4]. It's been five years," replied Lamis.

"Any kids?" came another question.

"No, not yet."

Hearing this, both the aunt's and niece's eyes popped.

"I looked at you, and I could tell there is something wrong. You look so pale and ill," Aunty revealed her prophecy. "I am telling you, juice one potato and cucumber, rub it on your skin every day. Within seven days, I guarantee you, your husband won't be able to recognise you. When Umaiza was pregnant, I told her to

---

3 Child.
4 A formal yes.

drink coconut water every day, put pictures of pretty babies on the wall and look at them all the time, but Umaiza pays no attention. Look at Taha's complexion, so dull, went on his dad's side!" Aunty got a bit carried away.

"Waisey, Phuppo[5] has a lot of totkay. I'm serious. My elder sister got pregnant just following her instructions," explained Umaiza.

Ten minutes into the conversation, Lamis's reproductive history had gained momentum. To divert the topic, Lamis asked, "I can understand hair and skincare routines might work, but do you really think these kitchen herbs and spices can cure diseases?"

"Why not? I have never been to a doctor in my entire life. I don't even know what they look like. Ma sha Allah, I am fit and healthy," replied Phuppo with pride. "Coming back to your pregnancy..." Phuppo didn't let it go. "Beta, you need to buy the root of a bohur tree and peel the skin of some reetha also. Now mash or grind these two together very well. Mix it in milk every night and drink. In fact, I would say give it to your husband too. You never know; you might end

---

[5] Paternal aunt.

up having twins." Phuppo clapped and laughed with enthusiasm. "Also, when you meet your husband..."

"I live with him. Why would I meet him?" asked Lamis innocently.

"Uffo[6], no, I mean, meet, meet..." Phuppo gestured, bringing the fingers of her hands together. "Just put a pillow under your hips."

The colours on Lamis's face changed from pale to red and yellow for a moment. She couldn't believe a total stranger was talking to her about something so personal. Out of respect, she just kept quiet, excused herself, and started calling her friends in hopes of escaping the conversation.

[6] An expression used to express excitement, impatience, or irritation.

Suddenly Taha started crying. "I told you to put some heing on his stomach. He is constipated," Phuppo told Umaiza off.

"But, Phuppo, it smells so bad, we have the wedding to attend today," Umaiza explained.

"The wedding is more important than your son? Let me go home. I will do it myself. You young girls just don't listen anymore. That's why you all suffer from so many issues." She turned from Umaiza and back to Lamis, pointing. "Is that your friend?" she asked.

"Jee," Lamis replied.

"Uffo, look at her hair. She is almost bald. Does she oil her hair? Tell her to boil ginger and mustard oil, then massage it into the roots of her hair. She should have done it at least a month before her wedding so that by now, she could have at least had better hair. Anyhow, it's never too late," advised Umaiza's Phuppo.

"Seems like your aunt is on a roll today!" smiled Lamis, a bit annoyed.

"Yeah, we call her the totka factory at home," replied Umaiza. To Lamis's relief, her bride friend, whose makeup made her look like a bad copy of Cruella de Vil in a gharara[7], was done.

"Do I look okay? I don't know. I don't like it. Something's off," asked the bride.

At first, Lamis thought of telling her how awful the job was done, but then, she decided to just go home for the sake of her own sanity and then figure out how to lighten the gaudy makeup job.

On the way, she did, however, decide to give bohar root and reetha a try.

[7] Long skirt like piece of clothing.

Social Media Species

In this day and age, social media is taken very seriously. There was a time when family, their values and opinions, did matter. Now, friends, family, and shopping is just a click away. Values and systems have left the drive, and memories are safe somewhere in a cloud.

Each one of us has a social media personality. Where some use it for imparting their worldly knowledge, others use it to provide hours of entertainment.

With the Internet in everyone's hands these days, and hundreds of platforms, how about we take a look at how some desi social media junkies use this power?

The New Age Influencers

Let's start with the category that occupies the most terabytes of the global network. Pakistan has a population exceeding 200 million, out of which at least half is likely to be that of the Influencers. The "gram" makes them do things they wouldn't have done otherwise.

When you take writing, researching, and web address out of the equation, Insta-blogging or influencing is born.

You find this sort scattered all over the Internet, trying real hard to somehow look better than their competitors and gain more followers.

This species thrives on the three F's: fame, filters, and followers. It keeps changing its niche to be accepted in the world of algorithms, assuming it's influencing mere mortals into making major life decisions.

The addiction of seeking validation and a desire to cut the 100M followers celebration cake prompts it to show all kinds of questionable talents on screen.

Some use friends and family to acquire the big numbers, some sob their way to prosperity. Some create fake fan pages of themselves, while some try numerous dance moves or sultry poses to get the "K" in the followers. A few also drop into a brand's inbox, asking for free stuff.

When everything else fails, this species attempts to secretly buy the followers and then hold a celebration party, hoping no one notices its tactics.

It does this with hours of "filtered" footage for the stories, and at least a thousand pictures, which are later meticulously edited and posted.

Its Instagram influencer profile category keeps changing, from content creator to fashion stylist and so on, depending on its confidence and the number of supporters. The ultimate goal is to reach the "Public Figure" status, a critical and prestigious place to be in, to raise the media card prices.

The Mua

Some are born with talent, some practice and learn their chosen art, and then some think they just have it in them, but don't.

There are three subcategories under this breed.

Influenced by established MUA's, this breed tries hard to post looks to gain some fans and maybe earn some money. Even with unblended makeup and terrifying colour combinations, it believes it is the best and does not attempt to learn the tricks of the trade.

Then we come to the makeup artists or MUA's, as the world calls them. This is a talented bunch that actually creates good content. It is inspired by the MUA's who made it big and earned reality show deals. It comes up with new challenges and seeks to somehow run ahead of its counterparts. This species has overpopulated social media to the point that it has become hard to pick just one for the job.

Next, a few want to be called something different, unique, that can prove that they are more capable and far more talented than the general MUA's. This overconfident variety finds its own acronym to go along with its name like MUD, GMUA, LA, MUG, etcetera.

The Instigator

You will find this species on all platforms. Also known as the Internet troll. This creature fishes for victims in the dark hours of the night. It feeds on ongoing disputes or lays down bait for others to argue over.

It has branched out from socio-political trolling and has taken nations' modesty, customs, styles, and trends into its own hands.

It makes sure to lust over, then comment on an individual's slightly tight clothes and teach a thing or two about spirituality, just passing by. After all, it believes God has bestowed unto it the highest sense in all categories.

Branching out, there is a type that prowls for people seeking approval. It leaves a nasty comment on others' posts. It then watches patiently, with its evil laughter echoing and lingering in the realms when one after the other more trolls join in.

And how can we forget the female species? With a somewhat provocative display of pictures, it lurks on the Internet to feed on others' insecurities or achievements. After all, women bringing women down is its mantra.

The Bodyguard

This species spends most of its time just stalking and admiring celebrities.

It hunts down and eliminates all negative comments and trolling to protect its beloved star. This creature is a counteractant to the Internet trolls. Its flattering comments quickly move him up the likeability factor. Don't you dare leave a nasty remark on its favourite celebrity, as havoc befalls when it gets angry.

The Mr Know-It-All

As the name suggests, this species believes it is the most intelligent creature alive on the Internet. It posts unsolicited opinions and arguments on its profile. Philosophical by nature, this creature has a tendency to argue relentlessly and often anger fellow beings.

It thrives on inaccurate or intriguing information, then opens a debate to satisfy its hunger for conflict. It is the saviour that believes the world needs its guidance and judgement over every matter.

The Tiktokers

Where TikTok in many Western countries is being used to impart knowledge creatively, in the desi culture, it has become an outlet for the once seemingly ordinary creature to present its lip-syncing talents to the world.

This is a relatively new kind of species. Evolved from the Insta bloggers, this creature has very quickly acquired a lot of internet space. It has attained true stardom from lip-syncing to Bollywood tunes and dialogues to dancing to explicit songs.

Labelling itself as a TikTok celebrity, it doesn't care who follows it or who comments. It's the number of fans that matters. Publicity, good or bad, all is welcomed.

The male species' is mainly seen donning a thick chain silver bracelet with bluestone, ankle-high, tight trousers, shirt buttons open to the navel, with a shaved chest, lip-syncing, head tilted to the latest Salman Khan dialogue.

Whereas the female tries hard with an over-the-top fashion sense and brands plastered all over to seduce its way into the follower's heart. Often seen twirling in its frock, the female seems to enjoy highly thirsty comments in its space. It leads by example, looking for controversies to feed on and faking engagements or marriages with famous celebrities to gain more attention.

The fans frequently get a chance to see the favourite TikTok self-proclaimed talented star through the promotional meet and greet events it holds.

Unfortunately, many younger fans get drawn into the cycle after seeing their favourite TikTokers achieving this so-called short-lived fame.

The Headless Vloggers

The name says it all. This species creates content for social media in an attempt to not be seen. There is nothing wrong with that, but the issue is that there are creative ways to shoot videos without just the torso in the frame. There is so much inspiration on the web that videos without a human element are also made possible. However, some of these creatures want to come into the frame to get famous but not show the head.

Surprisingly, the content is watched thanks to the desi curiosity gene of trying to get into everyone's lives. It usually talks about its daily events, shopping, cooking, and experiences without trying to be famous, i.e., taking the head out of the equation.

The Memer

This species is our primary source of entertainment on the Internet. Its brain works at the speed of lightning. It creates jokes, memes and insults on every thing that goes unnoticed.

In an effort to go viral, it works hard and provides us with entertainment all throughout the year. With thousands of Instagram meme accounts, this is one breed that is actually taking over the gram.

The Baby Boomers

Don't really have much to say. This species is still figuring out how to use social media and trying not to get into controversies by forwarding wrong messages around. It makes sure to earn one good deed a day by sending overly decorative "good morning" picture messages.

Next Door

Neighbours are people who help you adjust to a new locality.

Somebuild long-lasting friendships, and others come to the rescue when you are short of an onion, sugar, or dinner plates. On the other hand, mine gifted me with seepage and made sure that I leave the neighbourhood as soon as possible.

It all started with a leakage problem from the apartment on top of ours. It increased day after day and penetrated our apartment below. My husband and I were in the middle of our three-storey building.

I nagged, begged and flattered my neighbours above to look into the issue, but there was no solution. When I had given up, a very distinct lady emerged from downstairs, who I thought might be of some help, but God had other plans.

Her name was Zahida. However, she was popularly known as the "walkie-talkie aunty" within the compound because all she ever did was walk and talk. She was a short, chubby woman who, not only the grownups but also the children, hid from if spotted around the neighbourhood.

All she wanted was a walking partner, of any age, who would go round and round the buildings and listen enthusiastically to her issues in life. In short, she needed a charged-up energizer battery bunny.

Once, when I hardly knew about her, she stopped me while carrying my groceries home. She invited me to walk. When I excused myself, she started chit-chatting, and I politely kept smiling and listening to her.

Her conversation turned into almost an hour-long dialogue. I tried escaping many times, but she went on and on. When the butter in my paper bag was about to trickle, my husband, my saviour, my knight in shining armour, called, and I was set free.

Once, I was about to get into my car, and I saw her, clad in a dark green kameez, yellow shalwar, blue dupatta, and a maroon headscarf, approaching me in quick, short steps in her usual, boxy, manly, Nikes.

"You know there is a pipe leak in your apartment," she accused, then she went on. "The water is now penetrating my wall. I cannot do anything about it till you fix it. How much can I run around? You see, I am a widow." What I failed to understand was why she ended all her sentences with that last line?

I tried explaining and reasoning it out with her, but she was stuck to the point that our bathroom pipes were leaking, and we needed to break and redo them. She didn't comprehend the fact that the problem was with the bathrooms on the third floor and not ours.

Every single morning after that day was like a curse. It was either I would be caught by her when sneaking down the stairs or she would ring my bell. Soon, I had memorised her speech that would start my day.

Her solution: break the toilets.

My point: there was no point.

The neighbour's upstairs, the culprits of my misery, had turned a deaf ear, pretending to be oblivious to the entire situation.

Days turned to months, and if the bell rang, I had learnt to quietly sneak toward the door and peek through the eyehole without her knowing that I was inside. She tortured my house help and relatives when she spotted them pet siting my cat while I was away.

One after the other, she brought numerous plumbers to my residence to assess the fault and provide a solution. "This is Altaf. He is an excellent plumber..." she usually started by telling me how great her latest find was. Now another story is how they all ran away after spending a mere couple of hours with her.

Eventually, I decided that to get things done; I would have to adopt her way of annoying people to have them give in. I tried becoming the walkie-talkie's replica, but it didn't quite work for me. So, I became her wingman.

After walking more than a thousand kilometres with her around the compound, I finally pumped her into bullying the guilty party to look into the matter. My plan was a success. Soon the tenants upstairs fixed their pipes.

Or so they said.

The leakage stopped, but our torment didn't. She still insisted that we "break the bathrooms." Now she wanted to remodel her toilet and insisted that we separate our pipelines.

For her satisfaction and our eternal peace that I could kill for, I ended up "breaking the bathrooms" and separating the pipes.

By the way, it has been over two years now, and her washrooms have not been renovated yet.

As for the bathrooms above us, well, they still leak, and the water still seeps through our walls.

The Countdown Begins

The thumping on the door got louder and louder. Samar, Sara, and Kanwal sat in the storeroom, holding each other's hands, Sara sobbing profusely.

"Get a grip on yourself, Sara!" said Kanwal. "I've called one five, the police will be here soon."

Wondering what happened? Let's turn our clocks back a couple hours.

Kanwal, an A level student in Lahore, was visiting her maternal cousins, Sara and Samar, for a week. The three were just two years apart and inseparable since childhood.

Kanwal, a thin and dusky complexioned girl, was the wisest among both her cousins.

Samar was the same age as Kanwal and was often mistaken as her twin. She was usually reprimanded for playing pranks on her sibling, Sara, who was two years younger, petite, and the most naive of the three.

Khala and Khaloo[8], Mr. & Mrs. Zafar, had just left for dinner with their friends at the superhighway, around fifty minutes from their home. It seemed like it was going to rain. Since they had not enjoyed an evening out with friends in ages, they'd decided to carry on with the plan.

Where, around the world, youth indulge in creative or constructive hobbies, the desi youth somehow get their boost of dopamine from the jinn[9] or churail[10] stories. It's the favourite pastime when two or more friends or cousins get together in the evening.

If indulging, the story of the highly famous pechal pehri[11], the lady with twisted feet, definitely highlights the conversation. Surprisingly, every Karachiite[12] has experienced an interaction with this mysterious being known as the bride

[8] Maternal aunt and her husband.
[9] A supernatural spirit.
[10] Witch.
[11] A female spirit with twisted feet.
[12] A person living in Karachi.

of Karsaz first-hand or through someone they know. The story keeps changing, but people are convinced that she exists. Many social media pages and news channels have dedicated their spaces to this lady who roams around trying to hitchhike wearing a red bridal dress in the midst of the night. She has slowly gained more popularity than any influencer out there. It wouldn't be surprising to find her on Instagram endorsing brands to a few thousand followers.

No parent at home, the house help's day off, lights dimmed, and heavy rain set the mood to watch the newly released movie The Ring.

Sara was the timid one among the three. However, to prove that she wasn't a scaredy-cat, as the other cousins had named her, she mustered up the courage to get through the entire movie.

Samar and Kanwal decided to share a few horror encounters of their own to get that adrenalin kicking in before getting to the movie.

An hour passed. The plot thickened, and fear took over the room. Sara survived halfway through the movie, with her eyes shut most of the time, reciting all the prayers she could think of at that point.

There was one more hour to go, and suddenly their home phone started ringing in the lounge, timed perfectly with the scene of the phone ringing in the movie.

For a moment, all three froze in their places. Kanwal paused the movie, "Samar, go and answer the phone."

"You go. I'm not going to answer the phone," Said Samar.

"Okay, leave it. If it's important, whoever it is will call us on the mobile," said Kanwal.

The ringing stopped. Kanwal was about to hit play, when suddenly the phone started ringing again. "I told you to not talk about the jinns and demons so much tonight. I'm sure it's her!" said Sara with tears in her eye.

"Oh please, Sara, stop being silly. You think Samara is calling to tell us we have seven days..." Kanwal went quiet as the power went out.

The heavy rain had caused a blackout in their area. A widespread occurrence that almost every Karachiite is used to by now.

"Now what? Who will go out to switch the generator on?" asked Samar.

"What? the generator isn't automatic?" shrieked Kanwal.

"No! someone has to go out and switch it on," explained Samar.

"No way! I'm not leaving this room. One of you will have to go...." Kanwal was interrupted when the phone rang again.

This time it rang for a bit longer. Disconnected. Then rang again.

"Who can it be?" terrified Sara started crying.

"Let me call Ammi[13] and check. Maybe they're calling us." Samar tried to calm Sara down.

Someone started banging at the door.

It got louder and louder.

Stopped, then started again.

---

[13] Mom.

Samar had nothing to say to calm Sara down, who had gotten pale and was crying with horror.

"Ammi isn't answering the phone. Kanwal, what to do? I'm actually getting scared now," muttered Samar.

The phone rang again, this time along with the thumping on the door.

"I think let's hide in the storeroom and let me call the police." Kanwal led the two to the tiny storeroom attached to the bedroom and locked it from the inside.

It was warm, dark, and stuffy inside. Samar had turned on the torch on her phone while she kept dialling her parents' phones. Finally, their dad answered. "What happened, beta. I left the phone in the car, and mum's was on silent. There are at least thirty missed calls."

"Baba, there's someone outside our house. He's trying to break in. We're scared and hiding in the storeroom." Sara broke down. "No one was answering the phone. We have called the police."

"Stay in the storeroom. We're coming," said Mr Zafar. "Why didn't you call Asad? Let me call Asad to rush and check."

Asad was Sara and Samar's paternal cousin. Their uncle, Mr Zafar's brother, had recently passed away. Asad lived just two blocks away with his mum.

Fifteen minutes had passed, there was no sign of police or the electricity coming. The knocking and phone ringing had stopped.

After a while, the electricity got restored, so the girls decided to go out of the storeroom, as it was getting suffocating. As soon as they stood up, the door flung open. All three let out a loud scream with their eyes shut, thinking the intruder had come to get them, but out came a very familiar voice. "Sara."

"Mama!" screamed the girls with tears in their eyes and turned around to see the parents standing with Asad, who was drenched from head to toe, peering at them with anger in his eyes.

"I've been knocking and knocking on the door. I called so many times. I knew you guys were home. Why didn't you answer the door?" grumbled Asad with clenched teeth.

"What? It was you? What happened?" Kanwal asked, puzzled.

Mrs Zafar handed Asad a towel, asked all the kids to gather some composure, sit in the room, have some water, and relax.

She then explained that Asad's mum was travelling to her sister's house in Pindi, and he had locked himself out of the house. His cell phone's battery had died, and it was raining heavily on the way back home from work, so he was using his work phone to get in touch.

"So why didn't you call on our mobiles?" Asked Sara.

“Ohhh, so sorry, I’m not as smart as you!” replied Asad with a snide. “I called the landline as I don’t remember any of the personal numbers, and your home was the last non-office number I had dialled two days ago. It was raining heavily, there was a power cut, so the streetlights had also gone off. I knocked and knocked, then waited in the car, hoping that someone would respond.”

“Oh, okay, sorry, we thought someone was calling us to let us know that we have only seven days...” Sara began.

“Sara, please”, interrupted Samar, “let it go!”

Pride To Be

o, in our society, there are two "types" of marriages: Love and Arranged.

Then there is a kind for those who like someone but don't want to go through the process of wooing, courting, buying gifts, spending money, or admitting their love for that person: getting the elders involved.

Getting married is an ordeal in Pakistan; that includes a long process of finding the prospective someone who will be the right fit, not just for yourself, but the entire khandaan[14]. The brainwaves need to connect with each individual at their level.

Since many families live together, the rule above applies to a daughter-in-law more.

[14] Entire family including extended family.

However, if two people fall in love and are lucky, the whole process gets easier. Otherwise, they end up including the ordeal of getting the entire family to agree and validate their love in this already extensive love hunt!

Unless there is a dying wish of one of the grandparents to get the unlucky girl and boy of the family hitched.

So, let's get to our story.

Mrs Khanzada was a former principal of a college in her community. An ordinary-looking woman who no one ever recalled seeing smiling. She came from a humble background and had sworn not to reject any potential daughter-in-law based on looks. Ironically, she was set on a mission to hunt for a fair, tall, and slim girl who could look after the health and wellbeing of her one and only beloved son, Salman.

Salman, according to his mother, was the most eligible bachelor in town. A tall, dark, and not so handsome tech geek whose interests had led him to become a videogame developer. A career that is not very common in Pakistan. According to the desi standards, the only advantage was that he had managed to secure Canadian citizenship and worked at a reasonably well-paid job in Canada.

Salman's father had passed away right after Salman had flown off to Canada to study Computer Science. Since then, he'd made sure to visit his mum back in Pakistan every year.

For the past two years, the yearly visit to Pakistan for Salman turned into a rishta hunt. It started slow, casually meeting a girl or two the entire trip, to a full-fledged three girls a day, every day, momentum. The desperation had driven Mrs Khanzada to hire a cupid, matchmaker aunty, in at least four continents of the world.

Even with so many resources scattered worldwide, and so many marriageable options, Mrs Khanzada's search always ended in vain.

Either the potential daughter in law's family would get intimated with Mrs Khanzada's personality and interrogation, or she wouldn't pursue further as: *"larki ka rang saaf nahin*[15]*,"* *"is nay toh masters bhi nahin kiya*[16]*,"* or the famous *"larki ka qad kum hai, Salman keh saath sahi nahin lagey ga*[17]*."*

---

[15] *Larki ka rang saaf nahin* - Girl's complexion isn't clear.
[16] *Is nay toh masters bhi nahin kiya* - She hasn't even done master's.
[17] *Larki ka qad kum hai, Salman keh saath sahi nahin lagey ga* - The girl's height is less, won't suit Salman.

Days turned into months and then years, but not a single proposal converted into her dream of seeing her beloved son in the crisp white sherwani[18] that she had already shortlisted, the kullah[19] of which matched perfectly with the bridal jora[20] of her soon-to-be daughter-in-law.

Salman's disappointing marriage hunt got to a point where the poor lad had to pretend to be working on a weekend and later change his phone number to avoid the cupid arrows targeting him.

Once, he drove an hour to meet a family that eventually, like always, got rejected. The fewer the options, the more extensive Mrs Khanzada's list of qualities got.

So, finally, that time of the year had come when Salman would visit his mum and get caught up in the vicious cycle of the rishta hunt, leaving no opportunity to meet his friends.

Mrs Khanzada was eagerly waiting for her precious son. She was unable to go to the airport due to her monthly kitty gathering. However, Salman's favourite meal was prepared, and the

---

[18] Groom's suit (Pakistani)
[19] Turban
[20] Dress

diary to meet the potential brides was finalised. This time, Mrs Khanzada felt that she would find the right fit for her small family. The girl she was about to introduce her son to was not just a PHD in history, but also knew how to make precise, round rotis[21] as if measured by a compass. She was well-mannered, shy, slim, and tall. Mrs Khanzada had decided to compromise on the skin tone this time.

So, the car braked, the driver helped carry the luggage in, and Mrs Khanzada came rushing to

[21] Flat bread

the lounge. However, to her surprise, Salman was not in the room. Instead, there sat a dainty little Asian girl. She quickly pressed the palms of her hands together in a prayer-like gesture, slightly bowed, and sang a "Sawasdee kha."

Confused, Mrs Khanzada started looking around the room for Salman, who had disappeared somewhere in the kitchen. He came back, holding a glass of water.

"Beta, who is this?" Mrs. Khanzada asked.

"This, Mama, is Chaem Choi," replied Salman, a bit flustered. "We met two months ago at a friend's place. We liked each other. I wanted to decrease your burden and give you a surprise, so I married her last week! Also, she just finished her master's in math!" Salman exclaimed, looking at his new nerd bride with pride.

Now, how Mrs Khanzada eventually accepted her daughter-in-law is another story. Let's just say it took a lot of time.

Love @ First Byte

We desis believe in marriage, and dating doesn't fit our system. People prefer to let their parents live in oblivion than admit to going out with someone.

Even with all the norms and practices in place, the internet has discreetly helped individuals get into the dating world. It's keeping both the parents and kids happy, as youngsters get a chance to find a date while parents think they are looking for a soulmate on a rishta site.

Even though mail-order brides and seedy introduction sites have given a negative image to online matchmaking, when everything else fails, parents encourage their kids to find a partner online, hoping Cupid's arrow to be just a click away.

Where many have genuinely found love on the internet, several are still struggling to find a regular person online.

Why, you may ask? How about we look at a few profiles on the Internet marriage mart and see for ourselves?

Rizwan, 33

I am the eldest among my siblings. I have five sisters and a brother, all unmarried. One sister is doing an MBA. She is in her fourth year. Two are in University. One is in second year. Younger sister and brother are in school. My father is an A.S.P at a local police station. Mother is a housewife. We all live together.

I need a loving, caring, and romantic girl. She should be beautiful, outside and inside, and rich.

I am not looking for a Princess. She should not be liberal. Should have the courage to face the problems of life and the ability to stand beside me in difficult times.

Junaid, 25

My friends describe me as a funny, intelligent, caring, kind, bubbly person, sensitive at times, mature, confident, humorous, easy-going, honest, a good listener, flexible, considerate, charming, good-looking, engaging, organised, trustworthy, respectful, efficient, and reliable.

Looking for a girl who is funny, organised, a good cook, attractive, kind-hearted, religious, polite, smart, caring, loving, mature, thin, fair, optimistic, reliable, trustworthy, dutiful, honest, and efficient.

Her heart should be very beautiful, innocent, honest, loving, caring, and soft.

Amal, 23

I am a pretty young gal looking for a suitable match.

The guy should be a handsome, educated, generous, loyal, good-looking, and lively person. He should be well dressed and stylish, as I am very fashionable and want to see the same traits in my match. I want a rich and positive thinking husband.

Arif, 26

Its Arif here from Dubai, nationality Pakistani. I'm looking for a respectful, honest, lovely, and sweet like honey girl for a life partner. That's it for now.

Naveed, 38

I am an engineer. Working in Qatar. I am well settled and already married. I am here to network.

If all goes well, I will go for a second marriage.

I am looking for someone who will take my life to the next level. Serious, loyal, and cute girls, feel free to contact me.

I am like an average person. Not very demanding, a little careless. Trying to live a normal life. That's all.

Alisha, 22

I love travelling, that's why I'm looking for a nationality holder man. I'm also a foodie. I love street food, long walks, snow, and winter weather.

Thank God I'm beautiful, but I don't want a person to marry me because of this reason. I want someone who will first know my character, sincerity, honesty, and innocence and accept me as I am.

If I wanted, I could write stories about myself, but I want to see the person made for me first.

Ameera, 25

I'm a noble girl who belongs to a middle-class family. I offer prayers. I am friendly and cooperative and can live in hardships with my partner.

I want a loving, open-minded father-in-law, mother-in-law, brother-in-law, and sister-in-law who will love me and understand my love for them.

Looking for an educated and noble person with no kids. Someone who really wants to enjoy life in a halal and positive way.

Nasir, 28

Nothing is perfect. Life is messy. Relationships are complex. Outcomes are uncertain. People are irrational.

I am sharp-minded, independent, and confident. Nothing special.

Jimmy, 31

My sister is healthy. Please read this profile before proceeding. She is single and ready to mingle. If you wanna talk, please message me. We are also looking for my brother, aged twenty-five.

Sadia, 22

I believe in simplicity. I like engineers, especially mechanical and civil. I need someone who will make me feel that I am right; otherwise, everyone will feel I am wrong. I believe in sharing love, happiness, and respect a lot. I would like to settle in Europe.

Daniya, 35

My name is Daniya. I am currently in Dubai.

I'm a modern, open-minded lady and looking for the same. He must be from the upper class or upper-middle class. People with low salary, please do not send a message, or I will block you. Age should be more than thirty-seven. Must have his own house and be independent.

The Curiosity Shop

"Good morning, everyone. Flight 288 from Dubai to Karachi is ready for departure. Please switch off all mobile phones and ensure that your seat belt is fastened, your seat back is upright, and your tray table is stowed..."

I sat in my seat, a little excited but also a little intimidated at the thought of moving to Karachi. I was certainly not relocating for the neighbour's rooster who doesn't let you catch up on your sleep, the power cuts that eventually teach you the value of electricity, or the delectable local bun kababs, prepared in the most unhygienic manner but delicious enough to tantalise the taste buds.

It was neither the food nor the surroundings. My husband was taking me back to where I belonged.

My patriotic husband, after spending almost six years abroad, had finally decided to settle down in Pakistan. I, being dutiful, old fashioned, head-over-heels-in-love-with-the-husband-wife, was ready to do what was best for my significant other.

Born and brought up in the Middle East, I had never experienced living in Pakistan, though I remember vacationing in Karachi with my parents once every year during the summer holidays. It was a different feeling. You know you won't be there for long, so you tend to enjoy and take in every single moment that brings you closer to your roots. Vacations were always fun. However, I had no idea how different things would be when I actually lived there.

"Madam, could you please switch off your mobile?" asked the flight attendant, noticing a middle-aged, slightly overweight, gaudily dressed lady in pink sitting by my side with arms decked in gold as if she either owned a gold mine or smuggled from one.

The lady in pink went on without paying attention to the annoyed flight attendant, who was now almost leaning over the seat, going red with anger.

"Madam. Please. Switch. Off. Your. Mobile." She broke the sentence into words to get her message across. "It's for your own safety."

"Okay, I have to switch off the mobile now. Take care of yourself. I have kept the food in the freezer. You will have no problem, bye." The woman finally ended her conversation and smiled at the stewardess who walked away, shaking her head side to side in despair.

"Did you see how angry she got? She's so impatient. I think she has some personal domestic issues," whispered the lady in pink, turning her attention toward me.

"That's why, you see, girls should get married early..." She went on and on.

I was totally baffled by her hypothesis on the cabin crew's life and had no idea what to say when, "If you don't mind, could I please sit by the window?" she requested with child-like enthusiasm.

"Sure," I answered, faking a numb smile at her and adjusting to the limited space.

After making me feel uncomfortable with her frequent smile and stares, she finally inquired, "Are you married?"

I knew this question was in the pipeline but didn't expect it to come quite so soon. I could easily make out that her mind, like a matrimonial website, had already started screening profiles of possible grooms, digging out an ideal match for me.

"Yes," I replied and instinctively dreaded the next question.

"No kids?"

"No, not yet," I responded, hoping the conversation would end there.

"Okay, then you must be newly married." Her smile widened as if she had unravelled a complicated mystery.

"Well, not really. I have been married for ten years."

Her face changed. Her ecstatic smile suddenly faded away into a confused and inquisitive expression. It appeared as if she had seen an obnoxious ghost!

In our society, a woman married for ten years should have had at least three or four kids to prove normality in her life. I guess I was living most abnormally. A child is considered a blessing, and the 'childless' is deeply empathised with.

One after the other, her unending list of awkward questions began to pour. The more I loathed being pitied over my childless status, the more it victimised me.

Suddenly, a greeting interrupted her. I turned around to see my saviour; a delighted lady in green, who stood over my seat, dressed quite similar to the one sitting beside me.

'Naila!" shrieked the lady in pink in her piercing voice.

With sympathy in her eyes, the lady in pink first looked at me and then, to my horror, told her friend my reproductive history.

I wanted to sink deep into my seat and disappear. I thought it was just a nightmare, but no, I was very much alive and awake to see my childless status be publicised.

Their chat had just begun when the food trolleys appeared. The lady in green hungrily vanished somewhere among the rows of seats behind us, inviting the aunty in pink to an empty seat beside her.

The lady in pink looked at me with an even broader, guilty smile and asked if she could go to sit with her friend. My interrogation was about to end. I happily moved out of her way.

For the next hour, I felt like a prisoner just released and thrilled to feel the fresh air and see the world after many years of captivity.

At that moment on the plane, I decided to create a fake child for future inquiries, in fact children, the numbers mattered too! Pinky, Munna, Akku, and Timmy.

Rotten Eggs

hey say when life gives you lemons, make lemonade. However, what to do when life gives you eggs, and that too—rotten?

"Baji[22]!!!" came a loud cry from the lawn. "Baji, jaldi[23]!" screamed Rani once again at the top of her lungs. Zahra, panicky and clueless, ran toward the garden.

Zahra, twenty-five years old, was a home economics graduate, and recently married a marketing professional, Ahmed Khan.

They lived in a double-storey house with Ahmed's parents, who had still not retired and spent most of their time in the Middle East.

[22] Elder sister or used by house help in place of Madam.
[23] Quick.

The concept of having domestic help is quite prevalent in Pakistan. Every Pakistani household has hired help either living with them or coming in for house chores part-time.

Rani was Zahra's trusted house help. Two years ago, when Zahra had married and took over the Khan household, she'd come across Rani, recommended by Zahra's neighbour, Anum.

Rani had worked in the neighbourhood since she was a fourteen year old girl. Accompanying her mum, she went to all the neighbourhood residences and knew everyone in the colony. There was a point when Rani had taken on so much work that even she had to hire a part-time maid to clean her small cottage. Her dream was to marry Shehzada, a small garment store owner in the city.

Rani was a regular at Shehzada's store. Every first week of the month, she would spend half of her salary purchasing dupes of the latest lawn collections for herself.

The Khan's residence was in a well to do neighbourhood. Zahra and Anum had quickly developed an interesting bond; that of love and hate.

Zahra despised Anum and her frivolous ways, and Anum couldn't stand Zahra's immaturity. However, by the look of it, they were the best of friends. Inseparable and warm.

Now, coming back to the garden.

Rani stood at the gate throwing out something that looked and smelled like a century-old egg.

"What happened, Rani?" asked Zahra, huffing and puffing. She hadn't worked out in the longest time and coming down the stairs running toward the garden burned at least a few pounds.

"Baji, see; an egg!" she screamed. "It's a rotten egg!"

"So?" Surprised, Zahra just couldn't understand what Rani was trying to say.

"Baji! Why don't you understand?" cried Rani.

"What's there to understand? can you please stop panicking and tell me what's going on? You know I have an anxiety issue," Zahra told her off.

Superstitious by nature, Rani shrieked, "Baji, someone is doing black magic! Someone left it here, I am sure."

"Are you out of your mind? First of all, who would want to hurt us, and second, why? That too with an egg? Who does magic with an egg?" Zahra just couldn't believe what Rani was saying.

"Baji. I am telling you—it's baji Anum. She bought some quail eggs last week. I know," Rani explained. "I go to this very learned woman in my village. She does spells on eggs and passes them on. She wanted..."Rani got interrupted by Zahra, "One minute, why are you going to this woman?"

"Baji, you know I like Shehzada. He doesn't even look at me. I saw this ad on a wall, '*mehboob aap keh qadmoun mein*[24]', so I thought to give it a try," explained Rani.

Again, she was interrupted by Zahra, who couldn't believe what she was hearing. "Rani, Please throw this away and get back to work," Zahra ordered and left, mumbling.

Zahra was a gullible person. Even though she didn't believe in any taweez[25] or black magic,

[24] *Mehboob aap keh qadmoun mein* – Your lover at your feet.
[25] Amulet with spells or just spells.

when it came to Anum, Zahra was ready to accept anything.

The next day, again, into the bedroom dashed a bewildered Rani. "Baji, there is an egg!" she exclaimed. "I am telling you, baji, Anum baji is doing Taweez. There is a broken egg on the lawn," cried Rani.

"Rani, can you please let me finish this week's episode? Stop with these superstitions," said Zahra, half lying comfortably on the bed with the remote in her hand, watching TV.

That morning, Zahra watched TV but couldn't get Ranis's premonitions out of her mind.

An hour or two later, when Rani came into the bedroom to clean, Zahra casually asked, "Rani, why do you think Anum would do taweez on me?"

Rani, the storyteller, got an opportunity to chat. "Baji, whenever Anum baji goes to visit her sister's farm, she always brings some small eggs with her. I know there is this baba in her sister's area. He is popularly known as the '*andey waley baba*[26]'. I asked Anum baji to take me along to her sister's some time, but she never does. I am sure she visits that baba. Also, Anum baji doesn't really like you," Rani continued, making a goofy face.

"Really? What does she say?" asked the curious Zahra, who had started to believe in Rani's theories.

"She says you are immature. Also, you are fortunate you got a husband like Ahmed bhai[27]. Sadly, he can't leave you unsupervised, as you will end up doing something silly," Rani answered.

Zahra went red with anger and asked, "Does she say anything else?"

---

[26] *Andey waley baba* - A man who does magic through eggs.
[27] Brother.

Looking at her baji, Rani just made an excuse and left the room.

Rani's superstitions and Anum's remarks had already instilled doubt in Zahra's mind. Zahra started roaming around in the garden more often. Just to keep an eye on any suspicious activities happening around her house.

Though considered a sin, once, she even bribed Rani to ask the love witch for some sort of a remedy from Anum's spells. Zahra, by now, was convinced that something was not right. She believed she was losing more hair than usual and gaining weight. She had started avoiding Anum, would give a fake smile if accidentally they crossed paths, and would dump any food or gift that arrived from Anum's house.

One beautiful spring day, while sipping the afternoon tea in her garden, Zahra spotted not one but two eggs in a corner.

For a moment, she felt like there was no blood left in her body. Terrified and trembling, she slowly tiptoed toward the rotten eggs, making sure Anum wasn't looking from somewhere around the wall.

Zahra called the security guard and asked him to dispose of the cursed eggs and check how they had gotten there. In a few minutes, they both saw some movement around the bushes. Zahra and the guard went toward the shrubs, and to their surprise, they discovered a mommy quail staring at their faces while incubating her eggs.

"Arey Baji, birds push bad eggs out of their nests. So this is why we see rotten eggs around the garden!" explained the guard.

The Animal Within

They say that pets represent their owners. Even research has shown that many pups look like their owners and often share personality traits. So how about we head over to a posh neighbourhood and have a look around?

Pappu, The Feral Cat:

Notorious for being the dirtiest goon cat on the block, Pappu was often attacked by fellow cats of the colony and even the ruthless shop keepers and kids. The only human she trusted was the mohalla[28] sweeper, Amjad.

Amjad and Pappu shared a special bond. Amjad made sure to bring some leftover bread and milk for his friend every day when he came for work.

[28] Neighbourhood.

Sometimes Bakri, the street dog, joined them for supper.

Prince, The Persian Cat:

Prince, the stout and snooty kitty, now one year of age, was bought from a greedy breeder, who sold the tiny kitten earlier than usual.

His owner, Sana, had bought him for one purpose, to show and tell.

Sana, a housewife of a well to do business executive, wanted a cat for reasons even she didn't know. However, we do know that two members of her kitty group had recently adopted pets. The news had prompted Sana to hunt for a golden, long-haired cat. No other kind. The research took a bit of a time, but finally, Sana found her little Prince, held him up toward the ceiling, and screamed, "I got a Persian cat."

The next day, she made sure to call every friend and foe to tell them that she had "purchased" a "Persian" cat and was planning to take him to the spa. Any other breed was turned a deaf ear to. In Sana's world, buying a Persian cat was a status symbol. The adopted cats were looked down upon. Sana was up for a competition, and no non-Persian, non-spa going, or adopted cats came near.

Dojo, The German Shepard:

Dojo lived with a pack of German Shepherds at his owner's farmhouse, which was quite a drive away. He was recently brought to their house in the big city as he was the shyest of the pack, and the owner felt he wouldn't be able to cope with the others in the group.

Dojo also knew a lot about his owner and his dual life but could not communicate it to anyone else. Especially his owner's wife, Mona, who Dojo adored.

Dojo had seen it all, the farm parties, the alcohol, the guns, the dancing girls, one more wife of his owner, and then the family time at the same farm.

Mitthu, The Foul-Mouthed Parrot:

Mitthu had been living with his owner Zia for the past ten years. Zia's grandmother, may her soul rest in peace, had gotten the parakeet when he was really young. Theirs was an upper-middle-class family.

The grandma had a bit of an issue. She enjoyed swearing. Mitthu being with her all the time, had also learnt quite some vocabulary. It'd been two years since the grandma passed away, but Mitthu made sure he kept her spirit alive with all the curse words he greeted each guest with.

Bakri, The Street Dog:

Bakri in Urdu actually means a goat. Amjad found the dog scared, hiding from the kids who were throwing stones at him, near a pile of trash that graced the neighbourhood. The so-called educated and opulent people of the colony had two major complaints: the gathering piles of rubbish which they littered the streets with and, of course, street dogs.

Looking at how large the dog was and how much he resembled a goat, Amjad named him Bakri. Bakri was a bit moody and often enjoyed the food put out by the rescuers instead of joining Pappu for supper.

Justice, The Very Pampered Pomeranian:

Justice's owner, a very modern thinking, liberal girl called Lubna, got him from a certified breeder in the USA when she had gone to study there.

Liberal Lubna believed in equality and her right to choose. She mingled with the hip crowd, knew the right people to get her job done, had dreams, ambitions, and no one was competent enough to question her ideologies, not even her family.

Lubna's father, Dr Haroon, a famous ENT surgeon, could never say no to his one and only spoilt daughter. He made sure to provide her with the best of what he could.

After graduating with a degree in Liberal arts, oblivious to the fact that things were very different from when she had left, Lubna returned with her Pompom, Justice, in hopes to serve her country.

Little did she know that adjusting all over again at a place she had left five years ago would not be as easy as she had thought. Her views and personality had changed. What she felt was right was pretty wrong in culture. Now, it'd has been over and year. Justice and Lubna were still trying to figure out their lives in Pakistan. Lubna, however, had a shift of careers and ideologies. She developed a liking for Pakistani TV shows and was trying out her hand at fashion design. Dr Haroon wasn't pleased with her decision, but again, he could never say no.

Justice, though, not very happy with the groomers, was loving all the attention and the privileged life. He knew he was the prettiest dog in the colony.

Chotu, Baby, And Gigi, The Adopted Street Cats:

Bano had taken upon herself to feed and look after the strays of the area. A friend of Sana's, Bano, was against the idea of buying pets. She actively volunteered at a few animal charities and rescue centres.

Bano started feeding Chotu right under her apartment, later he got some friends, one of whom Bano named Baby. The neighbours and residents of the complex began complaining and nagging about the increasing number of street cats.

Many committee meetings and arguments took place, but Bano held firm to her beliefs.

There were even rumours of poisoning the cats, but scared of Bano's anger, no one had the guts to take that action.

Chotu and Baby started bringing dead rodents as presents for their knight in shining armour, and then slowly invaded her house.

With as strong a personality as her owner, Bano's fluffy rescue Gigi had still not gotten along with the other two. They couldn't trespass on her territory, and the same went for Gigi.

Sex Ed

In a society where sex talk is considered taboo, where TV channels are quickly switched over as soon as a steaming wet sari dance comes on; it's ironic to see aunties shamelessly gathering around a new bride, asking her if there's any "good news" the next morning after the wedding.

Eshaal, a young twenty-something-year-old art teacher, was about to get married in a week. She took time off from work, as Pakistani weddings end up with months of festivities. It's a joyous moment, as getting married and procreating is the sole purpose of our being.

With the wedding day around the corner, Munni khala[29], Eshaal's maternal aunt, was appointed to give her the sex prep talk, right after her Mayoun:

[29] Maternal aunt.

a day when the bride dons a yellow dress and is rubbed with ubtan[30] and God knows what other herbs and spices for that beautiful bridal glow just a few days before the big day.

Being the eldest among all her siblings and cousins and the first to be tying the knot, poor Eshaal had no clue what awaited her.

After getting done with all her Mayoun rituals, on Eshaal's mum's signal, the tired and sleepy bride was pulled into the small guest room by the very enthusiastic but shy Munni khala.

We live in a world where dating apps and every piece of information is just a click away. Still, Munni khala, as a custom, had taken it upon herself to educate and enlighten what she thought was her very naive niece.

Munni khala had been working up the courage to have this conversation with Eshaal for some time now. With the ladies still singing to the dholak[31] in the next room, clearing the throat, khala said, "So, you are getting married in a few days."

"Ahan," replied Eshaal.

---

[30] A yellow paste made with natural ingredients to give a glow to the skin.

[31] A traditional drum.

"Are you happy?" Came another awkward question.

"Of course, khala, we have known each other for over two years. I really like Amir," replied Eshaal, with her attention now entirely on her khala.

"Is Amir good to you? Do you talk with him every day?" Munni khala further inquired, thanks to the inbuilt gossip gathering mechanism.

"Is everything okay? Did something happen? Please tell me, khala. You are worrying me now," Eshaal asked.

"No, no... don't worry. I was just asking. Actually... I'm sure you know..." replied Munni khala, fishing for words in her mind.

"Know what, khala?" replied Eshaal, a bit agitated now.

"No, I mean, you're a smart girl. You've known Amir for so long. I'm sure you know what happens after one gets married, right?" Munni khala finally blurted out. "I mean, come on, I knew, and I'm not even from this age. Yet my Chachi sat me down and explained..." she continued.

"Oh my god, I can't believe this," Eshaal said with a palm on her forehead. "Are you trying to give me the sex prep talk?"

"Shhh... don't be so loud. Someone will listen," Khala warned with a finger on her lips.

"Khala, there's no one here. Plus, isn't this what you've brought me here in the room to talk to about?" Smiled Eshaal.

"Okay, so you know, right? Your mum just wanted me to confirm... and maybe give a few tips," Khala went on.

"I'm really interested in the tips," laughed Eshaal. "You can't even talk to me about sex, and tomorrow you will be the first one asking me for 'good news' and give me reproduction tips."

"Well, I do have some techniques. How do you think your cousin was conceived the first week of my marriage?" smiling boastfully, Khala said.

"Khala, please. I'm not interested in having kids right away. I want to travel with Amir. Plus, I don't understand why Ammi would ask you to speak with me?" Continued Eshaal.

"What do you mean?" a little annoyed, Munni khala asked.

"Don't you remember how you freaked out when I first got my period?" Eshaal explained.

"Leave that," Khala changed the topic again. "I went to the roadside market and got you some really nice, sensuous nighties."

For a moment, Eshaal didn't know what to say. She had so many emotions going through her. She didn't know whether she felt embarrassed or shocked.

"If you're free tomorrow, let's go together. We can buy some more lingerie. I've also seen some special perfumes and oils that attract the partner. I just can't wait for your baby to come!" exclaimed excited Khala.

"All I am hoping for is for you not to barge into the room the next morning with a pregnancy test," breathed Eshaal.

Suddenly, Eshaal's younger sister came into the room, interrupting the extremely uncomfortable conversation.

"Why are you guys sitting here? People are about to leave. Won't you come to see them off?" she asked.

"You go. Yes, we're coming," replied Khala and quickly hopped over to Eshaal's corner on the sofa. "Okay, if aapi asks, tell her we spoke."

"Okay, Khala," sighed Eshaal.

"By the way, I did want to tell you a few breathing exercises though that I had tried at that moment and worked for me," Khala said. "You just take short breaths if..."

"Ahhhhh, please, khala, this is not right. I am leaving now!" Shrieking, Eshaal got up and ran out of the room.

The Expat Bug

one!" beamed Hadia with joy after changing her social media location to Dubai, United Arab Emirates.

With many opportunities opening worldwide, expat living has become quite the norm. As an expat, you can either immerse entirely and enjoy the unique experiences that life offers or get intimidated by new customs, traditions, and cultures.

Just like any place, there are two types of Desi expats: The ones who go "Haww hai"[32] over everything that is a little out of their comfort zone, and those who forget their roots and traditions entirely and start emulating whatever

[32] *Haww hai* - A way of expressing surprise and disbelief. The word is mostly used by women from Punjab.

they see as if freed from a cage. Very few fall in between.

Zoaib, my cousin, a well to do young man, had just landed in Dubai with his wife Hadia on a new job. Just like many desis, Zoaib had been to UAE a couple of times before as a tourist. However, for Hadia, it was new. She had never travelled out of Pakistan. So this was different. It was real. It was exciting.

When venturing into new horizons, it's always better to read up and get to know a little about the new location you will be at. However, reading and researching isn't really the desi's strong point. We believe we are naturally bestowed with knowledge. Unless a celebrity has visited the place or the location has appeared in a movie, no one bothers looking it up.

The whole taxi ride, Hadia couldn't stop looking and admiring the high-rise buildings and the clean, smooth roads. They passed by the Burj Khalifa. She had never seen something so grand and magnificent in her entire life, except in movies, of course.

It was magical.

They reached their hotel room and settled in. After an hour, both decided to head out and explore the city, their new, temporary home.

Their social media feeds would be full of stories and posts of their new, exciting adventures and explorations every day.

A month later, we decided to meet up for lunch. I, as usual, the over efficient being, arrived on time. This was my second meeting with Hadia. She had left a good impression on my mind the first time we had met in Pakistan. She appeared to be a pretty simple and sensible girl then.

However, carrying a fake Gucci clutch and oversized Fendi glasses in her colourful frock-like blouse and skinny distressed jeans, she, along with her husband, strutted toward the table in her gold heels, casually smiling and announcing, "Sorry, I guess we're fashionably late."

I felt a bit underdressed in my regular jeans and top.

After exchanging a few pleasantries, Zoaib started talking about the new places that they had discovered, the history of the UAE, and how he felt he now knew everything about this place.

The accents had an expat twist to them. Their hand gestures had Arabised.

Whatever place I suggested, they either said they had seen it or behaved as if I didn't know much. They had become the Wikipedia of Dubai, just pompous.

Their confidence was beaming. I, the person born and raised in the country, started questioning my knowledge about the land. Maybe I didn't know much. Perhaps now things had changed. The meeting, though, left a lot of doubts.

Slowly, they made more desi friends who were similar. Their lifestyle and personality had changed entirely.

We met a couple of times after that, every time they looked different. Arrogance had started showing on their faces. New gadgets, cars, designer wear, and parties were the only discussions we had. I was always cut short when talking about the city. Of course, I kept forgetting they knew more.

We made a few more plans to meet, but as usual, they all got cancelled as the duo either had prior commitments, or our timings didn't match.

One day while browsing through Instagram, I came across their picture. The profile read, "Mr & Mrs Influencer," that's when I realised that the expat bug had bit and infected the couple hard. It was a hopeless case. There was no turning back.

About The Author

Born and brought up in the UAE, Sanober started writing for high-end lifestyle magazines in 2002. Her professional profile includes working as an editor at a leading publishing house in Pakistan and a publicist for a music artist.

With an eye for editing and knowledge of the publishing world, Sanober took the next step in influencing lifestyle and found a publishing company, printing two lifestyle magazines in UAE and Pakistan.

Besides being a foodie, an active organiser of a few local meetup communities like board gaming and language and culture exchange, she believes in a good cup of karak chai, long drives with music on and watching documentaries.

She lives in the UAE with her husband, son and two cats.

Review

"Our Idiosyncrasies by Sanober H. Irshad is a composition of twelve short stories, ranging across several topics. From the matchmaker aunty, with an eye to setting up any single person that crosses her path, to various types of social media users and online daters, overly intrusive strangers, and well-intentioned but behind-the-times family members, Irshad creates a wide array of interesting characters, sure to entertain.

Through these characters and events, Irshad provides an intimate look into culture. With a delicate balance of social commentary and humor, Irshad's satirical pieces give readers something to think about while simultaneously keeping them entertained.

Our Idiosyncrasies is beautifully crafted, intelligent, and an absolute pleasure to read.

With many colorful and fascinating characters, Irshad immerses the reader in culturally and socially relevant topics from marriage and procreation to curses and legends. Every character introduced in Irshad's flash fiction will almost certainly bring to mind someone from your own life, and shine a light on the sometimes bizarre and peculiar way in which we interact with one another.

As the title promises, Irshad delivers short bits of insight into these peculiarities and delightfully illustrates that across individuals, families, and even cultures, we all have idiosyncrasies. A fast-paced, enjoyable read, Irshad's stories will resonate with readers of all ages, genders, and cultures."

- *The Lost Chapter, LLC*

Lightning Source UK Ltd.
Milton Keynes UK
UKHW020630051021
391693UK00011B/2516

Bob bore, cyn codi, mae Ceridwen yn chwilio a chwilio am ei sbectol. "Ble mae fy sbectol? O, dyma nhw! Bore da, haul!"

Bob bore, wedi codi,
mae Ceridwen yn ymolchi.
Mae'n cofio brwsio ei dannedd.

Bob bore, wedi ymolchi a brwsio ei dannedd, mae Ceridwen yn plethu ei gwallt.
Mae'n gwisgo gwisg ddu ac yn rhoi esgidiau am ei thraed.

Bob bore, mae'n bwyta llyfr i frecwast,
llyfr wedi ei dostio, wrth gwrs.
Mmm, blasus iawn!

Yna, mae'n glanhau'r ogof
ac yn sgleinio'r ffenestri.
Mae'n golchi'r dillad
ac yn golchi'r llestri.

Bob dydd, mae'n cael llyfr i ginio
ac yn mynd am dro.

Ond, mae rhywun bach arall yn byw yn yr ogof gyda Ceridwen...

Corryn y pry cop ydy hwnnw.

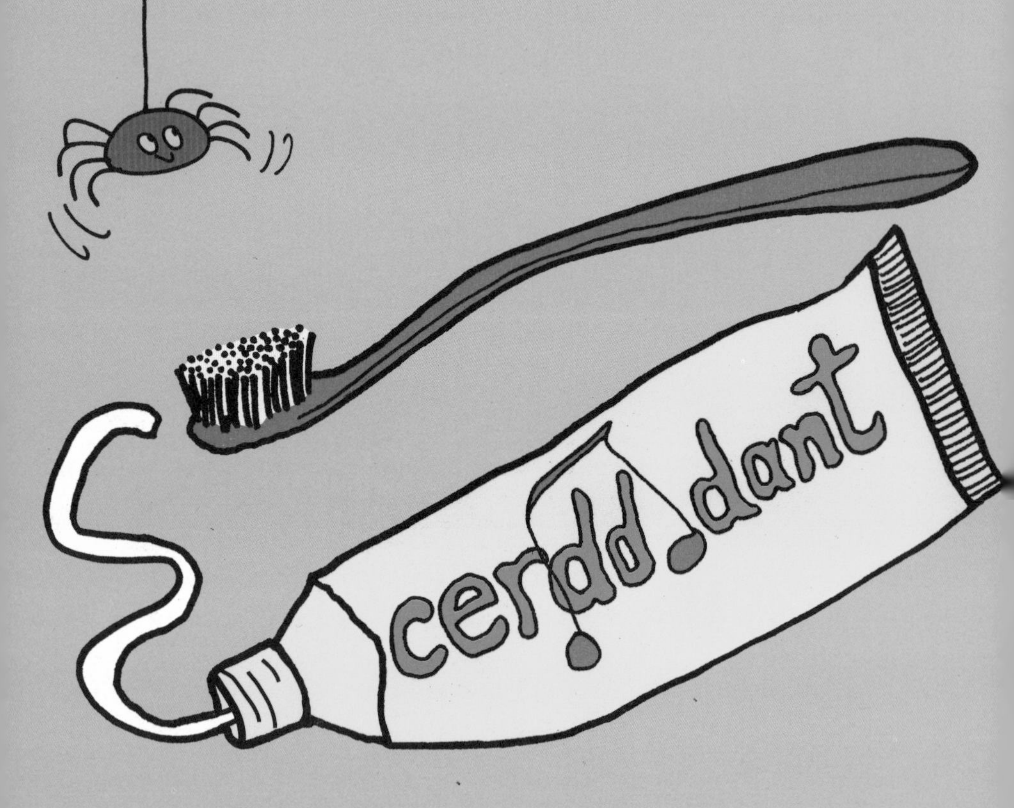

Dydy Corryn ddim yn ymolchi.
Dydy Corryn ddim yn brwsio
ei ddannedd.

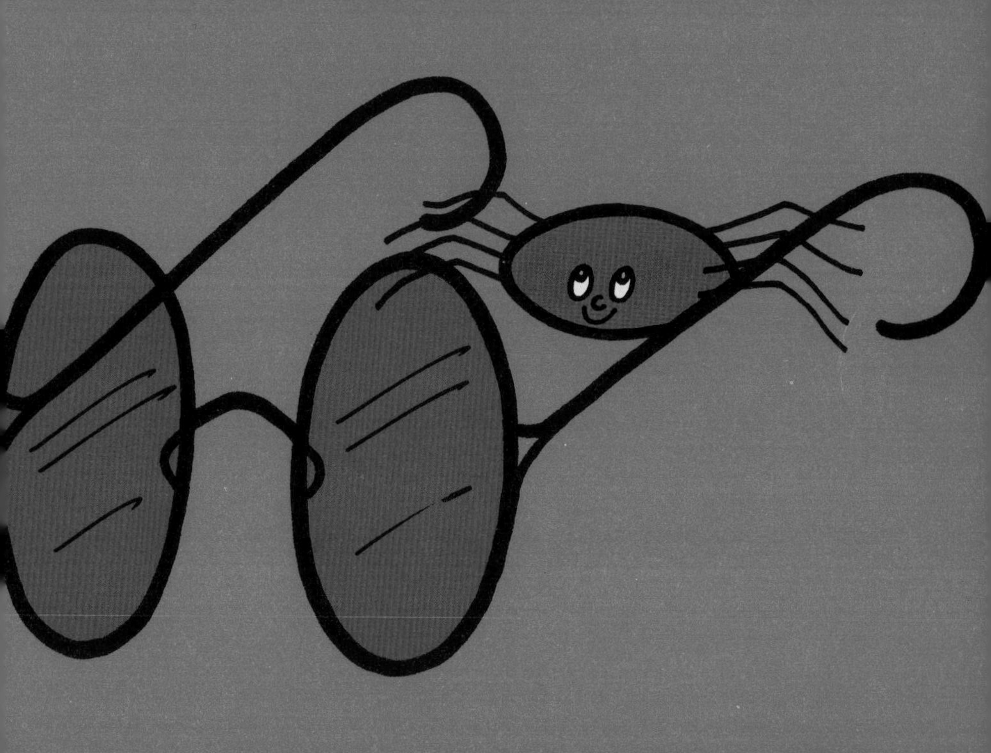

Does ganddo ddim sbectol.

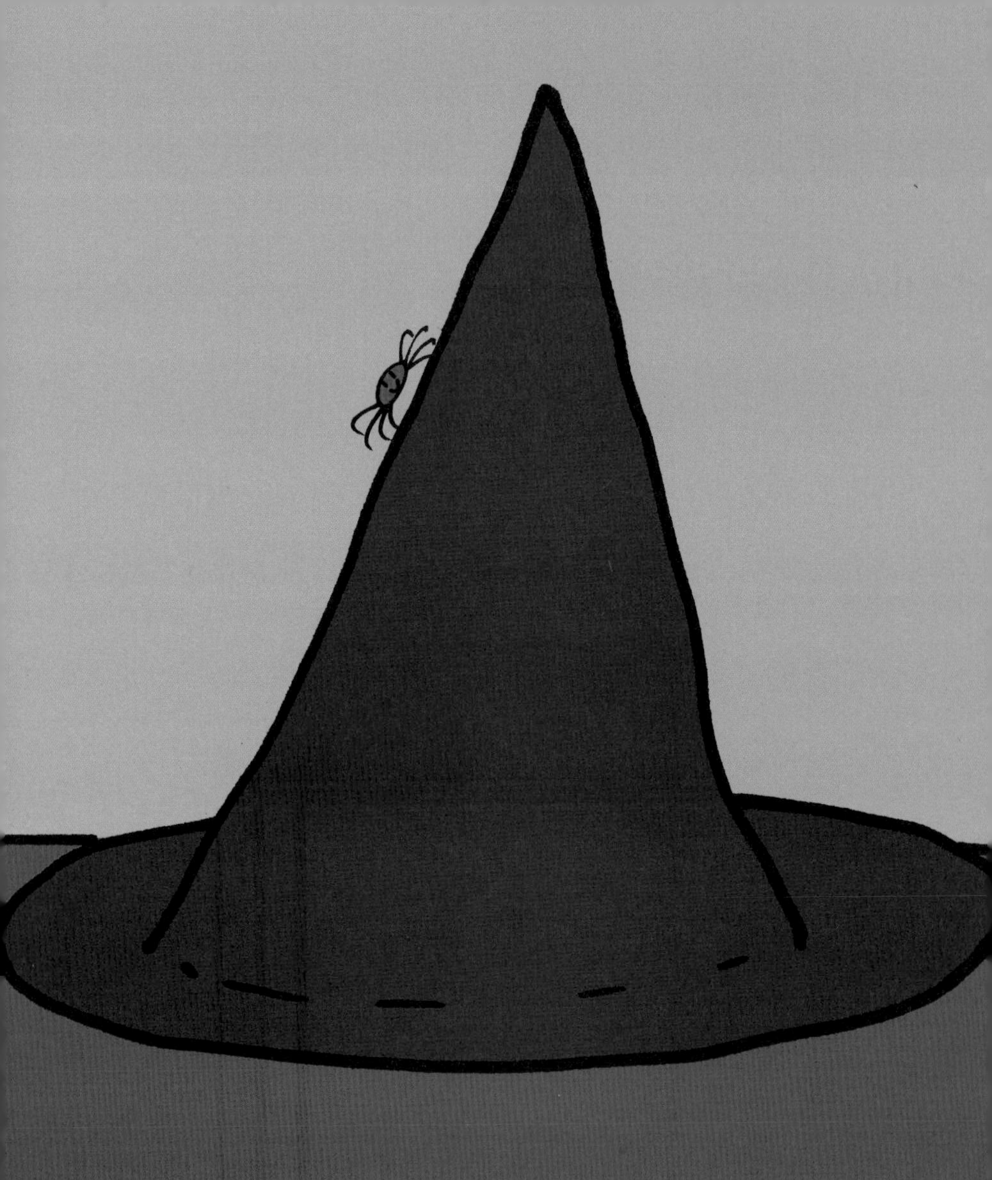

Does ganddo ddim dillad i'w gwisgo...

... nac esgidiau i'w rhoi am ei draed.

Dydy o ddim yn bwyta brecwast,
dim ond ambell i bry.

Dydy o ddim yn glanhau'r ogof
nac yn sgleinio'r ffenestri.
Dydy o ddim yn golchi'r dillad
nac yn golchi'r llestri.

Bob dydd, drwy'r dydd, yr unig beth mae Corryn yn ei wneud...

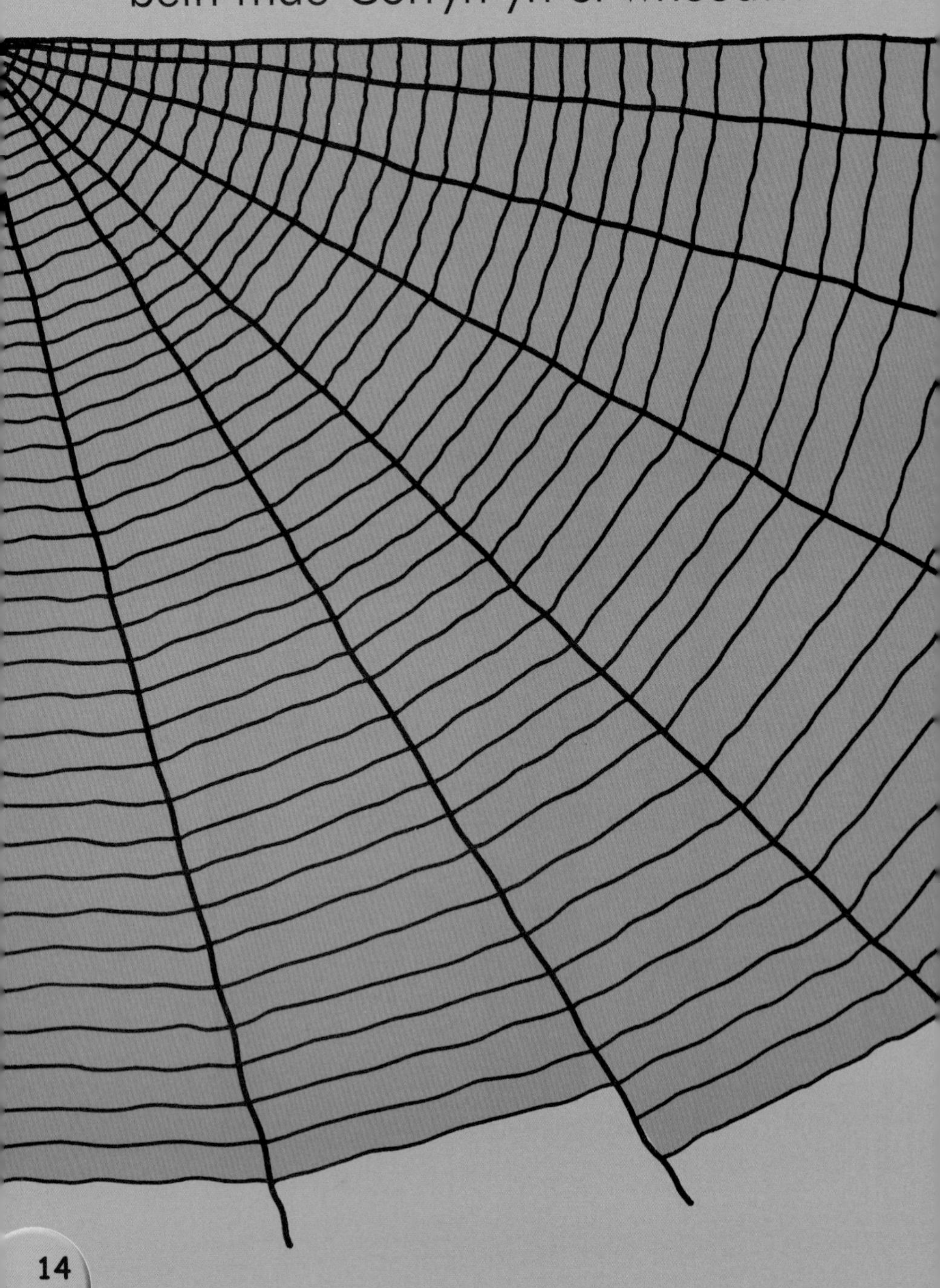

... ydy nyddu ei we.

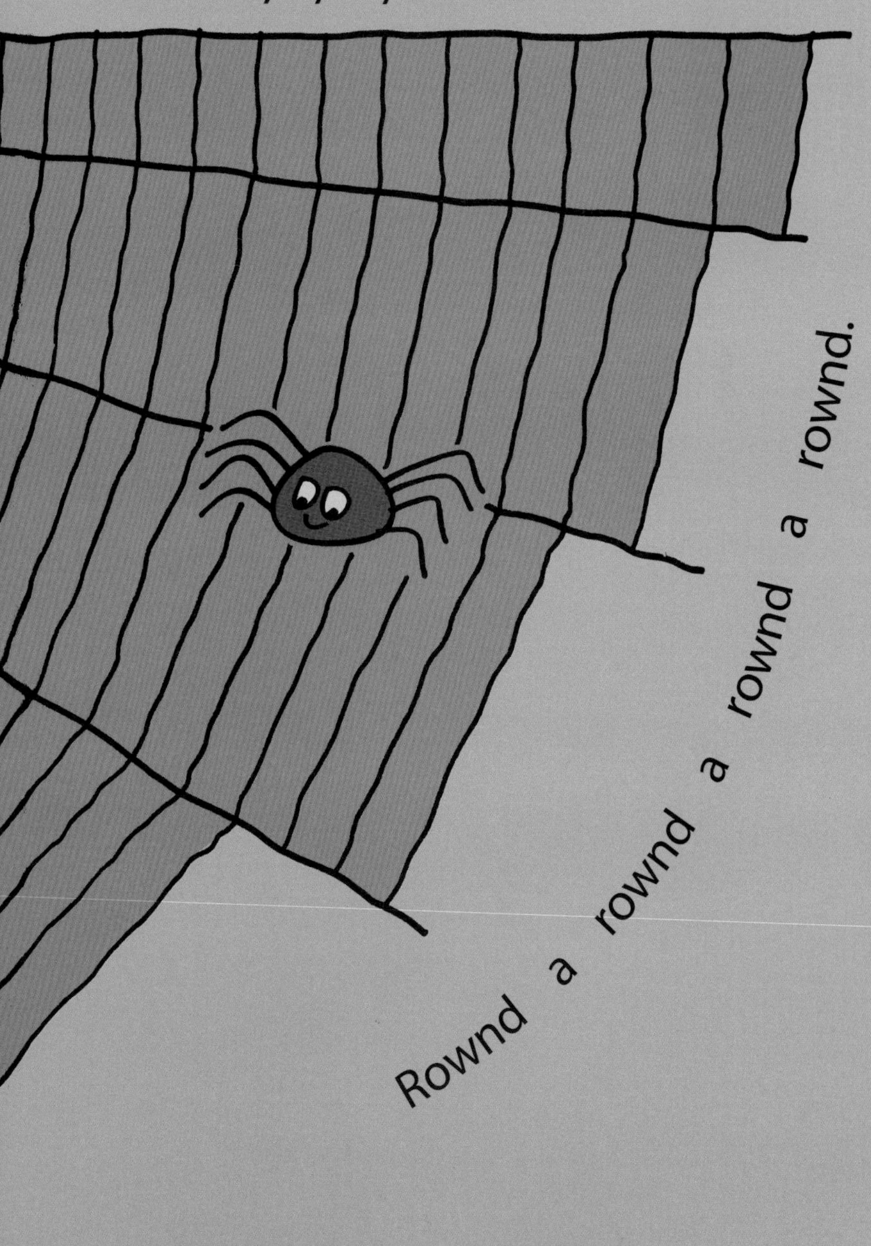

Rownd a rownd a rownd a rownd.

Un prysur iawn ydy Corryn.
Mae pawb yn brysur yn ogof Tu Hwnt.